From Donna·una
to Esther Mary.
Christmas 1930.

# TALLY HO

*a*

THE OLD MARE

# TALLY HO

## THE STORY OF AN IRISH HUNTER

BY
MOYRA CHARLTON

ILLUSTRATED BY
LIONEL EDWARDS

WITH AN INTRODUCTION BY
LORD LONSDALE

LONDON & NEW YORK
G. P. PUTNAM'S SONS

FIRST PUBLISHED, OCTOBER 1930
SECOND IMPRESSION, NOVEMBER 1930
THIRD IMPRESSION, DECEMBER 1930

Printed in England at
The Westminster Press
411A Harrow Road
London, W.9

# DEDICATION

I dedicate this, my first book, to my own darling Dad and Mum as a surprise, because it is to them I owe so much of my love of horses.

Moyra Charlton
*May* 1930

18th September, 1930.

*My Dear Moyra,*

*Thank you very much for the proof of the charming little book* Tally Ho *which you have written and sent me, and thank you also for the compliment you pay me in asking me to express my views on it. Although there are some sixty years between our ages, I think you possess a greater power of writing than I do, for your book is a charming one, delightfully written, and full of human feeling and instincts towards animals, and it is obvious that your love of animals has enabled you to compile this charming little book. The life of* Tally Ho *has so many human and animal touches in it that I feel sure it is quite unnecessary for me to express what I am perfectly certain all*

vii

readers of it will realise and love : your feeling towards animals is so well expressed, and the love of your horse, as you dream of him, is an excellent one.

I wish you every possible success with so delightful a book, which is so ably written, and hope that you may sell many editions of it, for it well deserves circulation. I wish you also every possible good luck throughout your life, and may your heart always remain open and tender towards the dumb animals we know and love, whose friendship we never forget, and who are the greatest and truest allies of man.

Believe me,

Yours very truly,

*Lonsdale*

# CONTENTS

## PUBLISHER'S NOTE

This life story of an Irish hunter was begun by Moyra Charlton just after her eleventh birthday and finished thirteen months later. She wrote it entirely without aid in her spare time, out of lesson hours. It contains many real incidents drawn from her own personal experiences in the hunting-field and in farm and stable. Moyra's father and mother read this story for the first time when it was in proofs.

# ILLUSTRATIONS

# CHAPTER I: *HIS ORIGIN*

The mare has now
Long gone to dust,
But still rests,
The old mare's foal.

OLD SONG.

THE wind howled across the desolate moor and the grey feathery clouds ran wild races in the tumultuous skies. Here and there a weather-beaten bush or puny sprig stood up in contrast with a bare grey rock or sheet of ice, and in less exposed spots sullen bogs were visible. The whole aspect presented a formidable appearance.

On the side of a small hill an old withered bush, of the kind I have already mentioned, sprouted out of a bare rock. By the side of this, knee deep in bracken and huddled up against the bush, seeking what scanty protection from the blast could well be afforded, stood an old black mare!

Her outline could only dimly be discerned in the gathering twilight, and a distant wayfarer might have taken her for a wild mountain pony or horse, so common in those desolate regions of Mayo and in the West of Ireland, but, advancing nearer, it showed that the mare had known better days and was superior, far superior to the common type of her kind. Her fine sloping shoulder, her good firm legs, her well-put-on head, all told the tale that old "Moorland Lass," for so we may call her, perchance once carried more than the coat of wool which she now wore.

I

B

# TALLY HO

The old mare stood shivering in the cold, but a sudden snort behind her made her turn sharply, and up cantered a handsome stallion. Though not so well formed, or with so much quality as the other, he was yet quite well made and above the usual standard. The mare measured about 15·1, but the stallion about 15·3 hands.

When the mare saw who it was she whinnied with delight, and the old stallion, well known to the folk around as Harum Scarum, came and stood protectingly over her as if to ward off evil, and Moorland Lass lay down in the shelter of the wizened bush to rest. At that moment a blinding sheet of rain fell and they were lost to view. . . .

Dawn's silvery fingers touched the dismal scene with light, lovely hands, presenting it, looking at its best. The storm had abated and in its place the sun rose, a ball of red fire, over the hill.

One little ray of light escaping from the others found its way down to an old gnarled bush, and beside it, as described already, stood the old stallion. But there was a marked difference in him as he stood with a vain attempt to arch his neck, his ears cocked at the least sound yet not slow to lay them back at the slightest offence, the sun glancing off his dark bay coat.

The mare lay as if fondling something, the picture of an anxious mother. Mother, did I say? Yes, mother—for beside her, and sleeping profoundly, lay a little black foal.*

* It is very rare that a foal is born grey. He is either black, brown or chestnut.

## CHAPTER II: *HIS FIRST DAY*

Curiosity killed the cat,
Satisfaction brought it back.

A PROVERB.

I CANNOT tell of the fun that foal had that day, of how he tumbled about on those four long stilts of his, of how he grew curious, over curious-looking stumps, and excited about exciting ones, of how puzzled he was about some things and interested about other things. But he was evidently enjoying himself thoroughly. Once his mother dislodged a pebble and it came rolling down towards him. The colt was frightened out of his life at this new horror and began to let out a series of feeble squeals. His mother, who was a bit higher up, on a small rise, whinnied anxiously. Blacky, for so we may call him for the minute, thought this noise sounded interesting, so he tried to do it too, but only succeeded in making all manner of comic squeals which sounded like a nightingale singing out of tune in the daytime. But after a time he got to do it very cleverly.

So the day passed very rapidly, and when the beautiful lights of evening changed from crimson pink to deep purple and the shadows began to lengthen, it was a very tired but contented little foal that went to sleep under the shade of his kind and watchful mother.

## CHAPTER III: *EXPERIENCE*

He grew and waxed strong.

LUKE.

**D**AYS passed, months passed, years passed. The poor slumbering little foal had grown to a strong, healthy, well-made, well-mannered, grey two-year-old, and indeed he ought to have done so, what with the good example of a watchful reproving father, and a careful, wise, and well-mannered mother, what else could he want? There was one thing—experience!

One day a strange pony came into the bunch with which he was grazing, for he could now eat as well as his mother. The older horses went up and sniffed at him and then turned away satisfied, but the younger geldings came up and tried to kick him.

The old pony turned round quietly, and said:

"Youngsters, would you kill an old horse of your own kind just because he cannot gambol and frisk about like you?"

They felt ashamed and turned to go away, only our friend hesitated. Perhaps he had a feeling of pity for the old animal.

"What are you dawdling about for, young colt?" asked the pony ungraciously.

The two-year-old stamped his hoof indignantly. "I am *not* a colt, and I am *not* dawdling, but . . ."

"But what?" snapped the other.

"But what made you so dejected and poor-looking?" at last ventured the grey.

4

HE WAXED AND GREW STRONG

"What!" exclaimed the old bag of bones with an angry toss of his head. "What! Why man, vile man, of course!"

"What is man?" asked the colt.

But the pony did not answer, and gathering up what strength and spirit was left in him, turned tail and cantered off. At that moment the mare whinnied, and when the grey came up to her, he asked:

"What is man?"

His mother looked at him softly and tenderly, but only said:

"Son, you may know some day."

And being *really* only a colt he did not mind whether he would know or not, so he just gave a little snort and trotted off after his mother.

# CHAPTER IV: *HIS FIRST SIGHT OF MAN*

All the world is beautiful
But only man is vile.

AN OLD HYMN.

OVER the damp early mists that clung to the bogs and the moist ground the sun rose with splendid magnificence, shedding its warm glancing rays into every nook and cranny, spreading joy and brightness wherever it travelled. It was not least appreciated by a small herd of wild ponies grazing on the shaded slopes.

A keen east wind was blowing, and the oldest member of the bunch, a fine stallion (the grey's father), threw up his head and sniffed the keen fresh air. He sniffed again and gave a little snort, but soon put down his head and went on grazing as if nothing had happened. Old Harum Scarum was too cunning to make a to-do about that! A little later a handsome iron grey lifted his head and sniffed. It was our friend the former Blacky. But even he, inexperienced as he was, did not seem over excited about things and started grazing again.

After a time a rattle of cart-wheels was heard on the rough stony track, and a solitary turf-cutter was seen winding his cautious way across the bog, standing in a ramshackle cart and clicking now and then to his shaggy donkey.

Suddenly, as if by magic, every head in the bunch was raised and every little ear cocked in that direction. The leader swung round, and with a whisk of his tail and a toss of

6

A SOLITARY TURF CUTTER

his head as if to say "I'm not frightened, but just do it for exercise," galloped off with the whole herd at his heels.

When they had slowed down the grey came up to his mother and asked eagerly:

"Why did we run away?"

"Why, from man, of course!" retorted his mother, with a "what else would we run away for" sort of air. She had been rather grumpy all the morning since a cheeky young filly had nipped a nice bunch of clover that she had had her eye on.

"Man?" he repeated in a puzzled voice.

"Oh, run away and play and leave me alone," exclaimed his mother, aiming a savage nip at his withers.

"All right," replied the grey, skipping out of her way with a hurried hop; then he arched his glossy neck proudly and went round telling all the other colts: "I've seen man to-day, have you?"

"And you will see a good deal more of him before your life is ended I expect, young feller," interrupted the stallion, coming up at that moment.

The youngster did not quite understand. "But I thought it was only for exercise."

"What?" snapped the stallion.

"That gallop."

"Oh that! Of course it was only for exercise," he agreed. And they moved away.

# CHAPTER V: *A GALLOP FOR FREEDOM*

Swift as an arrow—fleet as a deer.

A BALLAD.

IT was a bright spring morning in May, and the birds were building their nests and the air was pure and freshened by the constant showers. The great Mayo bog stretched for about sixty square miles to the left, and some lonely rocky hills, their summits wrapped in the early mist, rose from time to time from the vast expanse of waste, inspiring rather a feeling of awe and depression than a feeling of admiration for their grandeur and gigantic bulk.

Then of course there were the more fertile spots, where green grass even sprouted out of unyielding earth instead of the ordinary brown tufts or still more ordinary barren ground.

In one of these parts by a small grove of hardy trees a stallion was grazing a little way off from a herd of horses. It was indeed a pleasant place with the stream tinkling and gurgling laughingly through the shade of the trees, where the flies did not enter in such numbers and the shade afforded coolness and protection from the heat of the oncoming day. It was sheltered by three hills and therefore deeply resembled a small valley. Yes, it was indeed an ideal place for a horse.

Suddenly the stallion threw up his head uneasily and turned round and trotted back to the other ponies, then back he came again and pretended to graze, but in reality his lips did not touch the tempting grass. He had been fretting thus all the morning, and he had evidently something worrying him that he could not get out of his mind. His restless behaviour got on the nerves of some of the more highly strung of the herd, and the result was that at noon the whole lot of them were wandering listlessly about refusing to graze.

At about three o'clock things began to happen, things that were going to change the grey's life completely, for you may by now have guessed that he was of the group of horses. Suddenly through the clear still air was heard a long low whistle, then from the other hillock it was returned, sharp and distinct, in answer.

The stallion started up bewildered, for the "rounding up" of the ponies was held in the autumn, not in spring, but still his sense of duty out-weighed his minor fears. He neighed shrilly, and that neigh went to the heart of every horse; they knew what it meant—danger!

It was now of all times they looked helplessly up to their leader—they knew him—they trusted him with the simple faith that none but animals can know. Men wonder and plot —horses believe and obey.

Then what a hullabaloo followed: mares whinnying anxiously for their foals; yearlings losing their heads and rushing about knocking other horses right and left; veterans calmly forming into a circle; while the stallion trotted around trying to get the frightened youngsters into some sort of order. Then the thud of horses' hoofs was heard behind, and shouting; they did not need to turn to see who it was, they knew—man.

Off they set at full gallop in pretty good order, but after about a mile they began to string out a bit and some mares and foals were beginning to drop out exhausted. Let us leave them to their fate.

9

The grey was in front from the start, and was going strong, stretching his beautiful limbs to their utmost, his long neck eagerly extended and his mane and tail tossing wildly in the wind—clearing the ground with that long, steady stride of his which in later days was to distinguish him in the hunting-field and on the racecourse. But he had still a long way to go. No doubt he was afraid—yes, he was terrified, but that did not stop him from increasing his pace; in fact, terror lent wings to his hoofs.

From then on the noise rang in his ears—he had a confused idea of shouting, the thud of hoofs, the wind surging past him, and of having caught up with the stallion. Now they were even, neck by neck, stride by stride in a headlong race for freedom. They swerved round a bog, skirted a hill, a boulder stood in his way and the grey took it in his stride. They were going at such a furious pace that their hoofs hardly seemed to touch the ground. The earth grew harder and firmer. A great gate loomed up ahead; it was wide open—Harum Scarum steadied himself, made a desperate swerve to the left, righted himself and scampered away. The grey who was going too fast to check himself dashed through the opening. The gate closed behind him and he was caught!

# CHAPTER VI: *CAPTIVITY*

In the golden lightening
Of the sunken sun . . .
The pale purple even
Melts around thy flight
Like a star of heaven
In the broad daylight.

SHELLEY.

H E stood still, his heart thumped madly, madly against
his sides, the sweat trickled down his heaving flanks,
his nostrils were filled with blood to their rim, and the froth
fell from his lips into large white pools. His scratches and
cuts, where the brambles had torn his glossy coat, burned
pitifully, and the dark red blood mingled with the dripping
sweat. Yet he heeded not these!

The evening drew in and the air became chilly. The
golden sunset glowed and finally flickered out. Yet he
moved not. He stood stiff and still, his lips were slightly
parted and his eyes had a far-away look. How noble were
those thoughts that were passing through his brain. Something of a higher and nobler nature than man can reach. As
a well-known writer has said, "All horses are fit for heaven,
but few men."

At last he snorted. Gradually life and warmth seemed to be
returning and with them his power of observation. He looked
about him.

The sky was the colour of dark velvet, but an orange line
along the horizon marked the spot where the sun had dis-

11

appeared. He was in a long field; at one end ran a small river surrounded by trees; at the other end was the gate by which he had entered. In the distance a little white cabin was just visible, snuggling in a group of trees, from which a thin blue line of smoke found its way out into the fast darkening sky. And yet far beyond stretched the great brown desolate bog—so far off now—that had once been his home. He turned in the other direction. He was not the only occupant of this strange world. There were also three colts, a young stallion, and a filly from his herd besides a few dull heavy wagon horses.

The sky grew darker still, and one by one the stars came out. A bird twittered sleepily and then silence. So, overcome by tiredness he lay down and had soon forgotten his troubles in sweet and undisturbed slumber.

\*     \*     \*     \*     \*

The next morning dawned bright and clear. The whole of nature seemed happy and rejoicing, and how could our friend, bewildered as he was, not rejoice also? At least it was true that when he arose refreshed, even if he were a little stiff from his long sleep, his thoughts ran in a decidedly more cheerful channel than those of last night. For, however depressing the circumstances, youth cannot long remain miserable. Why? He was young and active, there was a new world to explore, he could kick anything that got in his way, and he wanted his breakfast.

This last he espied in the corner near the gate. Piled up against the wooden fence was a big bunch of hay which the other inmates of the field were already disposing of with satisfaction. So off he cantered with a playful bound, for he could not bear to be left out of anything.

And so the day passed. He frolicked with his friends, enjoyed himself thoroughly, and even the grumpy old cart-horses did not grudge him his hour of play. In fact, one of them became so amiable as to tell that "young bounder," as they called him, a few important things about the house and its inmates.

It belonged to some sheep farmers who owned a good many of the horses in that part of the bog.

The general "rounding up" season was, as Harum Scarum had thought, ordinarily in the autumn, but this year the horses had been taken in early, so as to be in time for some of the summer fairs. The most part of them he sold unbroken, but a few he kept for his own use.

"He is not a bad man," concluded the wagon-horse, "though he cares little for us, and profit is his chief aim. But take my advice, youngster, and claim Tom, the stable-boy, for your friend."

"But what about the master? Is he nice?"

"Personally, I do not take much notice of him. We get plenty to eat and only go to market once a week; what else do you want?"

"But," persisted the grey, "your life is different to mine."

"Well, then, you are nothing to do with me."

Then he, being unused to so much talking, turned away and proceeded to graze in silence, and the grey went to romp with his friends, though he had a feeling at the bottom of his heart that his lot was not to be that of the old shire horse.

\*    \*    \*    \*    \*

Three days after this conversation, in the early evening, six men came into the field with ropes in their hands. When they had got within perhaps a hundred yards of the horses they split up into different directions, two to the right, two to the left, and two kept straight ahead. Gradually they forced the group of frightened animals into a corner, then one of them advanced with a rope halter in his hand.

Our friend, who up till now had been watching the proceedings with a mixture of wonder and astonishment, finding himself on the outside of the circle, turned on the intruder and aimed a savage kick at his leg.

He missed, but it was lucky for him that Providence had chosen Tom, the under-lad, for his first intimate acquaintance with man, for beyond a muttered, "Begog—he's the deevil!" the man advanced with courtesy enough.

When he had got within two or three yards of him the terrified horse swung round and stood facing him angrily. This was Tom's moment. With a quick and skilful movement of his wrist, he slipped the halter over his head, and the unlucky grey found himself once again caught in the clutches of man.

# CHAPTER VII: *A TRAIN JOURNEY*

All the sights of the hill and the plain
Fly as thick as driving rain;
And ever again, in the wink of an eye,
Painted stations whistle by. . . .
And here is a mill, and there is a river:
Each a glimpse and gone for ever.

ROBERT LOUIS STEVENSON.

WITH great difficulty and no little resistance he was at length conducted, or rather dragged, into the small, dirty, but homely stable-yard.

The last faint rays of twilight were glimmering through the tall trees, and the chickens were pecking around in hopes of finding a few grains of corn or perhaps an egg-shell or piece of potato-peel. A pig grunted somewhere in the background.

The small, though slightly stuffy box into which he was led, had a cosy, comfortable air about it, even after the wild life he had been leading. It was lit only by a rusty stable lantern which flared up when the door was opened and the cold night air entered. Some cobwebs clung to the ceiling and a black beetle paraded the manger.

Soon Tom went, and the young horse was left to accommodate himself and his thoughts to his new surroundings.

Next morning when he awoke the birds were singing merrily and the cocks were crowing. A ray of sunlight filtered through a crack in the door, and he noticed a pail of water and a pile of hay against the wall. The water tasted horribly

15

of duckweed and slime, so he promptly knocked the pail over and stepped on it. Then he turned to the hay. This last tasted sour and musty, and so, being rather hard up for food, he decided to eat his bedding.

At about 10.30 his master came to see him. He was a harsh-faced man, and having made a few remarks about his mane and tail, and having said something about "the station" and "5.30, mind ye have him there," he went out. Farmer O'Neil was a man of business, and wished to dispose of the horses as soon as possible. From then on till four o'clock the grey was left to eat his bedding in peace. The top part of the door was open, and he liked watching the chickens and the cart-horses lumbering to and fro. There was also a small grey donkey whom he took a fancy to, and to whom he had the impudence to whinny, but he only received a loud ugly "HEE-HAW" in return.

At four he was fished out. Tom came to halter him, and before he knew where he was he found himself among two colts, the filly, the donkey, three cart-horses, also two pigs, six ducks, four turkeys and I am not sure how many chickens. These latter did not accompany the others to the station. It was not far across the fields, and with the others our favourite behaved fairly well, but when they arrived on the platform, and an awful dragon came shrieking, shouting, tearing, grinding past him, his nerve gave way and he bucked, kicked, reared and did anything that came into his head. He sat down on some luggage, put his foot through a cabin-trunk, backed into the waiting-room, scattering porters and passengers right and left. At last he quieted down into a sort of wide-eyed trance, and he was shoved into a van, but not without kicking a porter through the ticket-office. The train shunted off and he was not very surprised to find the earth moving under him, for if his manger had turned into a dragon he would not have been astonished now.

And so when at last the train came to a standstill and he was led out through the long street of a busy country town to some second-class stables, he was nothing loth to lie down on the damp straw and refresh his weary limbs with sleep.

# CHAPTER VIII: *THE NIGHT BEFORE THE FAIR*

Show me the way t'go home,
I am tired and I want t'go to bed,
I had a little drink about an hour ago
And it went right to my head.

SONG.

THE following morning the grey did not go out, and he was glad of it, for he felt stiff and aching all over, and he had developed a bad cough.

Wriley, the stud-groom who had accompanied him and his companions in the train, felt he deserved a day off, so he spent the whole morning and all his money in betting and gambling, and the whole afternoon and everyone else's money in drinking their healths at the "Lobster Arms," a dirty low type of pub. in the town.

Meanwhile, in the damp, low, wooden-ceilinged little shed where the young horse was stabled, the hours dragged slowly by. The dank straw and unhealthy atmosphere were telling on him. He was no longer the fine, active horse that he had been a few weeks ago, although he stood just as straight and arched his neck just as proudly as before; his ribs stood out through lack of condition, and his coat looked staring and dull. He was no longer the healthy gelding whose coat shone like silk; his eyes had lost some of their lustre, and a new look had taken the place of the old glance of fearlessness and fun—a look that betokened nervousness and dread. His cough had increased since the morning.

Round about five o'clock a boy thrust in a bundle of hay

which was not fit to eat. The shadows lengthened and it
grew dark inside the dismal little stable. But still Wriley did
not return. The grey had long since drained his bucket of
water to the dregs, filthy as it was, and his lips were parched
and dry. It got damper still, and he had no rug or blanket to
keep him warm, and he shivered all over. He paced restlessly
up and down the shed. Outside it had started to drizzle.
Would Wriley never come?

At last! Footsteps and voices! Down the alley they came,
about six of them, rolling and swaying, singing some rollick-
ing Irish song. They were clearly all drunk. Would they
stop at his door or proceed up the street? In his anxiety he
let out a shrill, penetrating, pitiful neigh. They paused outside his door and waited a moment in silence. At last someone spoke, and the high-pitched, disjointed sentences could
hardly be recognised as belonging to the sober-minded
Wriley.

"Here, will the baby come to Mither. Sure an' where be
his dhrink?"

A small shrewd man stepped forward.

"Where all yer dhrink goes to, Paddy Wriley," he replied,
with a meaning wink.

"Och man! he be arfter . . ." hissed Wriley, turning on
him; but the rest was lost in peals of laughter from the
others at this coarse joke. When it had subsided a bit he
said: "What d'ye mane, Tim O'Brian?"

"What ar says, an' ye can naht git out of it."

"Bad cess to ye," muttered Wriley with an oath—he could
not help feeling that he was getting the worst of it—"ye
better be arfter havin' the feeding of the bruht thin, eh?"

"Ar will naht," returned Tim, withdrawing hastily.

"And you, Patrick O'Conneley?"

"Catch me afther him."

"And why naht?"

"He has a whicked oi on him," he whined.

Wriley went the colour of a beetroot to his ears, and he swore a good deal. Everybody laughed and jeered. He eyed Patrick through the corners of his narrow eyes. He was a tall, big-boned, broad-shouldered fellow, while he, Wriley, was but a small, puny man, and his knees bent outwards, the result of spending most of his life in the saddle. But what he lacked in stature he made up for in courage, besides, those pints of beer at the "Lobster Arms," which he had so unwillingly left but half an hour ago, made him feel hot-headed and brave, so he turned boldly to O'Conneley and said mockingly:

"You be afeared, Patrick O'Conneley."

For reply he got a cuff on the ear, after which a regular tussle began, the others not wanting to be left out of the fun, and they all went off shouting, swearing, and fighting, followed by a crowd of enthusiastic street-boys, while the poor horse never got his water after all.

"HE HAS A WHICKED OI ON HIM."

## CHAPTER IX: *A HORSE FAIR*

With a gee-whoa here
And a gee-whoa there,
And here a gee,
And there a gee,
And everywhere a gee.

FROM "THE FARMER'S BOY."

NEXT morning the stable-yard was up with the lark, for it was the day of the fair. The weather had not improved since yesterday. It was still drizzling wretchedly, and the sky hung sullen and heavy over the busy scene. Stable-boys were darting about everywhere with dandy-brushes, curry-combs, rubbers, etc. Grooms were hurrying hither and thither with saddles over their arms, and horses were stamping, snorting and fidgeting about in their stalls. A stray dog had stolen into the yard in hope of procuring a dead rat or mouse, and was now giving tongue vigorously. The whole had an air of mysterious and suppressed excitement about it.

A boy entered the low, bad-smelling stable and started brushing the grey down, while another brought in some hay and water. Wriley did not appear, for (and this was only known to the horse long after) he had been arrested for "brawling in the streets" on the previous night with Patrick O'Conneley and a few others. Tim and the rest escaped, but their poor unlucky companions were sentenced to "five days of the best," and you may be sure they enjoyed it!

But to our friend. After the grooms had gone he did not eat his hay, the corners of his mouth were too sore, and he kept on coughing, coughing. It was very bad, all this, and he didn't understand it.

In about half an hour someone else came in, threw a halter over his head and an old sack over his loins and led him out.

Outside it was almost worse than inside. The yard was muddy and dirty; it was cold and the wind was now driving the rain wildly around. He felt miserable and depressed. The sleet beat into his face and frightened him; it beat down his throat and choked him; it made him horribly wet and the great drops trickled down his legs to fall into the slushy mud. Not that he was not well used to bleak winds and driving rain; in fact, on the moors it was much worse where there were no tall houses to protect him. And yet, hardy as he was, he shivered; it was all so different here.

A boy was summoned to take him. He was a little chap of about nine, who hardly came up to the grey's chest. He wore a pair of old discarded darned grey trousers which were three sizes too large for him, a ragged old coat with a hole in the elbow, and a cap put on the wrong way round. He went unshod.

The yard was full of noisy horses, young and old, who made it quite difficult to reach the gate. The small boy nearly got knocked down twice, which did not add to the comfort of his charge; but he struck forth again with surprising boldness, his only grievance being that he had lost his cigar-end. But when at last they did get on to the main road, and dropped in behind the long stream of horses and trucks on the way to the fair, it was beyond all bearing. Horses were slipping up everywhere on the wet asphalt, the road was crowded with herds of sheep and cattle, besides carts, drays,

BUT NO ONE SEEMED TO FANCY THE GREY

caravans and, worst of all, motor-cars. The young grey had never seen these before and thought them very terrible. Once he heard a "HONK HONK" behind him; he shied to the left into a dust cart and cut himself on a piece of rusty tin. Then followed words between his boy and the driver, until a civic guard came along and told them to "clear out" as they were blocking the traffic. So they had to move on, shouting at each other all the while (and I think, but I am not sure, that the small boy got the best of it).

So when at last they arrived at the big field outside the town where the fair was to be held, it was a very frightened grey horse and a very exhausted urchin that retired to a secluded corner and awaited the turn of events.

The fair was one mass of noise and colour, and the shouting of many voices droned into a distant hum that rose and fell like the rising and falling of the waves. Horses were whinnying, trotting, galloping, kicking, backing, rearing—in fact, horses were doing everything they should or shouldn't do. Foals were running away and tearing round with tails in mid-air in great excitement, to the amusement of all watching and the embarrassment of their owners. A band was braying some popular tune, and motorists were hooting and demanding where they were to park their cars. Now and then a sentence of conversation was overheard and then lost again amid the din, such as "I tell ye agin, he's the best horse in Ireland." . . . "Man, what are ye afther thin, ye could not get the like of him." . . . "Oi tell ye oi——" . . . "Here, boy, where can I put my car?". . . "Ye-es, she's a grand filly." . . . "A soft day, eh?" and so on.

Everybody seemed to be buying around, but no one seemed to fancy the grey; some people came up and looked at him, beyond that nothing seemed to happen.

At last a buyer appeared in the shape of a sporting farmer from the South; a good chap who could ride to hounds or quaff a pint of ale with the best of them. Farmer O'Hagen had a little to do with sheep, a little to do with cows, a little to do with horses—in fact, a little to do with everything. Best of all, a few pounds in the bank, for a better or more hearty fellow could not be found.

He had come to the fair to purchase an old gentleman's hack which he intended to buy cheap and then sell for double the money. The dark grey coat against the light green background of the hedge caught his eye. Now this good farmer had a soft spot in his heart—in spite of his mission—for young horses, and just out of curiosity he went up and talked to the boy about the price.

"Fefteen pund, yer honour," whined that worthy, and then, brightly in hope of a tip, "he would carry ye grand, that he would." This with a knowing shake of his head.

"Done," exclaimed the farmer, much to the ragamuffin's dismay, for he saw beneath the staring coat, stuck-out hips and vile cough the makings of a good lightweight hunter.

"It's a deal o' money for a poor man to give," he murmured as he turned away, "and the missus won't half be afther me for it, but," he added, while a flush of satisfaction crossed his face, " 'tis worth it!"

# CHAPTER X: *SCHOOLING*

Labour for learnin' afore ye grow old,
For learnin' is better nor silver and gold!
Silver and gold it will vanish away,
But learnin' itself it will never decay.

PATRICK MCGILL.

WE will leave it to the imagination of the reader to recount the horrors of that train journey and the rightful surprise of the "missus" on seeing a nervous young horse dancing up the lane instead of the "guaranteed quiet" gentleman's hack. But it will suffice to say that on arrival he was led into a fairly comfortable stall and given a good rub down and a bran-mash. He had never entered a stall before, but it was so nice and passably clean that he could not grumble. Besides, he was quite worn out by the excitements of the day and soon fell asleep.

The following morning, as the grey was having breakfast, he heard a whinny next door, and putting his head over the wooden partition as far as his head-collar would allow, he saw a fat bay pony of about 14·2 hands eating some corn.

"How do you do?" he said politely.

The bay pony ignored him and went on crunching.

"Good morning," he repeated, louder, feeling slightly puzzled.

The bay pony looked the other way.

"I said HELLO!" roared the grey, angrily stamping. He felt both annoyed and hurt.

25

The bay made no movement.

Goodness knows what would have happened next, but at that moment a big black horse peered over at him from the partition on the other side.

"Keep your hair on, old chap; you can go on yelling at him till to-morrow night," was his placid comment.

"Why?" demanded the young horse.

"Because he is deaf," was the crushing retort.

"Oh!" said the grey, feeling decidedly stupid, and as there seemed nothing else to say he returned to his breakfast.

Later on in the morning the master came to see them. The other horses liked him very much. They said he was very kind and gentle, and that he always had a nice bit of carrot or apple in his pocket for them. He seemed pleased with his buy and came in to pat him, and the grey, in spite of himself, did not mind it.

"Wot shall we call him?" he asked his wife that night.

"Ah!" she said, laughing; "Paddy, afther ye, eh?"

"Right you are," he replied, and returned contented to his pipe.

I might as well mention the rest of the stud. The bay pony was called Brownie, used chiefly for harness work; but he did not do much now on account of his age and deafness. The great black horse was called Sweep. He was of a very stubborn temperament, and had a mouth of iron; he had the record of "near pullin' the arms arf" four different owners for four seasons running. He was well up to eighteen stone. There was also Greylegs, the donkey, besides Billy and Mike, the two shire horses.

As day by day passed Paddy's manners improved, his cough disappeared, the cut on his quarters healed, he grew round and healthy, his coat got back its former gloss and his spirits revived. He also lost his dread of man, and began to look upon him as a companion and a friend. And happy days those were too. Sometimes he was let out into the pretty clover paddock with the little brook babbling gently through, and sometimes he was led along the green lanes by the under-boy, where the blackthorn and wild rose bloomed and the sweet smell of the honeysuckle laid on the breeze, and the air was filled with bees and birds and butterflies and thousands of tiny insects. And sometimes again he was put out with the other horses and sheep and cows into the field, and in the heat of midday they would all crowd under the shade of the elms by the ancient ivy-grown ruin and talk; or in the cool of the evening at sunset they would stand together by the old mill-pond and swish their tails at flies and listen to the birds.

But this could not always last. One morning he was brought in, and by petting and coaxing a bridle was at last got over his head. He did not like it, and showed his feelings in more than one way. The straps worried him for he could not shake them off; the nasty hard bit and the reins hanging at each side of his mouth hurt him. He did his very best to get rid of them, but finding nothing happened he gave it up and allowed himself to be led a few times round the yard before he was taken in. After, came the saddle, but that was not half so bad, and in time he got accustomed to both.

At last one morning a nasty heavy thing was fastened on to his back. Men called it a dumb jockey. He was lunged in a circle with a long rope; it moved about, and though he kicked and plunged it would not come off. This annoyed him more than ever, but it was of no avail as he soon found out.

Then, a few days later, the farmer himself came down to

27

the stables, and the stable-boy held his head while the master mounted him. At first he jumped about, but after walking a little way he became wonderfully docile and steady. Suddenly he whipped round, gave a buck and a plunge, and tore away.

His rider was ready for him and kept his seat, but in spite of all his efforts nothing would or could stop the horse, and when they came to the iron gate into the field where his friends were grazing he just shortened his stride, cocked his ears, and hopped over like a bird. He stumbled on landing, but scrambled up and dashed towards his companions when he came to a full stop.

And so day by day he learned and thrived. He was schooled over the little bank into the field to such an extent that he jumped out one day and was just seen in time by the boy. He enjoyed jumping the big gap in front of the shed as well, for he was a natural jumper. And as the winter approached he was taken in to be got ready before the hunting season began.

# CHAPTER XI: *CUBBING*

There is colour in the woodland as far as eye can reach,
Pale gold upon the elm tree, and bronze upon the beech,
To witch the world with beauty a hundred hues ally—
But bonniest is the scarlet when a whip rides by.

FROM "SCATTERED SCARLET."

IT was a dark September morning and a light frost lay on the grass. Dawn was faintly breaking in the east, but as yet no animal life had stirred. There was no sound except the gentle rustle of dead leaves and the regular beat of four hoofs on the hard slippery road which rang out in the cool still air. The rosy hues of early sunrise glowed for a moment on the dark tree-tops of a small grove of pines. Then a distant cock crew. The new day had begun.

The grey was feeling in the best of spirits; he had been wakened up in the middle of the night and fed and groomed by lantern-light. He was now on the road early, and was going out for some fun. That was all he knew and cared. Anyhow, when a pheasant got up at his feet and flew away with a "whir" into the trees, he gave a hearty buck, arched his neck and felt pleased with himself. With Farmer O'Hagen it was the other way. He seemed anxious about something, and kept on taking out his watch and muttering over and over again something about "bein' late" and all the "fault o' th' missus," etc. And at this point he would give the innocent Paddy such a dig with his heels which would send them both spinning along at a good sound pace.

29

By this time they were approaching a small knoll of trees by a fork. As they paused, wondering which way to go, the faint sound of a horn drifted across the early white haze. Paddy pricked his ears and listened; he thought it something wonderful, beautiful, and yet he knew not quite what. Guided by his rider's hand he took the road to the left, went on for a bit and then entered a gate on the right into a grass field. The spongy green turf seemed to say to him "Gallop!" and the fresh breeze seemed to say "Come along, race me if you can!" All his wild instincts awoke. He cantered up a little hill, possessed by a strange quivering excitement that made him tremble from head to foot.

As he topped the rise the sound of the horn came again, clear yet distant. Then what a view met their eyes! Here, there, and all around was a mass of colour. To the left an evergreen wood that stood silhouetted against the fast lightening sky; to the right a wood of silver pines intermingled with those of the copper-beech, ash, etc.; and most lovely of all, far, far below, the tangle of colour in all shades of yellow, brown, green, bronze, gold and amber, known as the Kilmallock Wood, and very indistinct was seen a few moving patches of pink and a white blob, probably a horse against a darker background.

It was a perfect picture, and Paddy stood fascinated for fully a minute, the light breeze just ruffling his mane. He had a heart, a big one too, but also a wild one, and in him grew a sudden longing for company. He threw up his head and whinnied loudly. For a time there was no sound, but at last faintly, very faintly, he heard the music of the hounds, the sweet note that so many horses get to know and love. This was too much, and without even a snort of warning he bounded forward into the valley.

But his rider held him in, talking gently to him all the while, and though he strove and fought against the bit, he found himself unwillingly complying with his rider's wishes. They trotted down a narrow grass lane, crossed a ride, skirted a covert, and finally hopped over a small ditch into a grass field. Once he felt the good sound turf beneath him the farmer "let go," and they raced away and galloped as Paddy had never galloped before, except on the day of his capture. Oh the joy of feeling the fresh air rushing to meet you and the green grass fleeing away beneath your feet! And this time it was joy, not fear, guiding him.

The country was well banked and fairly hilly, and when they came to a gate and squeezed through it into a lane—for every gallop must end however glorious—they suddenly heard the horn quite close to them, and the next moment the hounds came jogging round a corner with the hunt-servants in pink and gentlemen in various kinds of rat-catcher following behind. The next turn of events happened in a second. The grey was backed into the hedge—a hound ran between his legs and he kicked at it. The hound rushed round on three legs, yelping and howling for all he was worth. Paddy thought it a clever shot, but the huntsman evidently did not think so by the bad language which followed. The young culprit, now thoroughly frightened, launched madly into the crowd, and it was a full ten minutes before he settled down.

Now they had approached a small spinney, and the field waited on one side of the covert while hounds worked on the other. A few came up and spoke about Paddy to the farmer. One gentleman in particular seemed very interested and asked a lot of questions. He was a small dark man with kind but very sharp grey eyes, and a firm determined mouth. He was

31

mounted on a powerful bay and the farmer took off his hat and called him "sir."

"Well, Mr. O'Hagen," he concluded, "I like the horse, so if ever you want to get rid of him you will know where to send him to, see?"

Farmer O'Hagen thanked him very much and promised to consider the offer.

At that moment the loud baying of the hounds increased. There was a rustling of dead leaves, and a little red animal crept out of the bushes near by. Everyone shouted and waved their arms. The little creature looked behind him, hesitated, and the hounds were on him.

The farmer got a pad and seemed very pleased. On the way home he chuckled and slapped his sides; he had a "pint o' ale" to look forward to.

And as for Paddy, well, home and a mash were enough.

# CHAPTER XII: *A NEW MASTER*

Oh! give me the man to whom naught comes amiss,
One horse or another, that country or this, . . .
Who calls not each horse that o'ertakes him a 'screw,'
Who loves a run best when a friend sees it too.

FROM "HUNTING SONGS."

IT all came about like this. Paddy had had four days more cubbing and shown himself off much better than formerly. He was now having one of his last "days out" in the big field before the winter really set in. It was a cold day and he and his friends had been having a race to keep warm. He came off victor as usual, and as he was trotting past the gate, picking up his hoofs well and arching his neck, proud of his victory, he noticed a stranger standing there on a gaunt bay horse watching him. It was the same gentleman who had admired him on his first day's cubbing.

"Great Scott!" exclaimed the latter. "What paces and speed! I will get that horse by fair means or foul! Hello, here comes Mr. O'Hagen. Well met, sir, you are just the man I want!"

"Gran' day to yer, yer honer," gasped the farmer, running up. "Oi saw ye a-coomin' in, an' oi says to meself, says I, 'Sure, an' wot is it ye're afther?' "

"Well, Mr. O'Hagen, to be truthful, I am 'afther' that grey of yours. I have been watching him, and I want to buy him. Now what do you say to fifty guineas?"

"Och! that would be givin' him away to yer, it would.

33

D

Look at him now, sich speed, sich strength, yet so dainty, he'd take an ox thro' a china shop, he would. So I be gettin' fond of that little hoss, I am, an' so I be thinkin' . . ."

"Come along, now, none of your tales; what do you say to a hundred guineas?"

There was a pause, but at last Paddy's master, as if loth to let the words pass through his lips, said slowly:

"Will ye take him for a hundred and fifty guineas?"

"Done," cried Paddy's new master heartily.

"Done," echoed his old one.

And the two men then solemnly shook hands and went away. Thus the bargain was completed. And Paddy romped away in the happy sunshine in blissful ignorance.

But indeed he was lucky, for Major John Smithfield was one of the best masters in the countryside. He, on retiring from the army, had bought a large manor-house in the centre of a good hunting country for himself and his little daughter of eight, as he was a widower. He rode like lightning to hounds, did quite a bit of steeplechasing, and was tremendously popular in all sporting circles. But though he was always very kind and civil to his friends, his heart really dwelt with his daughter and his horses. Nevertheless, his unerring keenness and really sporting nature won the hearts of all around.

Next morning the groom was sent to fetch the grey horse. It was a cloudy day, but the sun shone in between the racing clouds, cheerfully, into the old yard. The farmer and his wife came to bid him farewell and brought lots of nice apples and sugar and all sorts of good things. As Paddy was crunching these happily, he wondered what all the fuss was about. He had been groomed very well that morning, and now his grey coat shone like silk. He was a five-year-old now and full

15˙2 hands, so he felt very grown-up. Then as the groom mounted him to turn away, the farmer stepped forward and gave him one last pat, and with rather a broken "So long, Laddie" still ringing in his ears, he turned away and clattered merrily up the lane, leaving naught but the ancient farm and heavy hearts behind him.

They had twelve miles to go, and it was not until early afternoon that they entered the large tidy yard with rows of boxes and stalls on each side. They had had a good canter on the way over, and the groom, Atly, rode very well. This made it pleasant for both horse and rider, and as the day had turned out fine, Paddy arrived in very high spirits. He was led into a cool, clean, airy box, with some nice fresh bedding on the floor, some lovely sweet water in a bucket and crisp hay in the manger. There was also a bran mash which he ate, but after that he walked round and round his stable, exploring. It was fitted with electric light, and the door looked out into the yard. This was very tidily swept and there were no chickens pecking in the dust.

At that moment someone came up, opened the door and exclaimed:

"Hello! here he is!"

Paddy looked round slowly, and standing there in the doorway he beheld his new master. He walked a step forward and cautiously thrust out his head. His master stroked it. For reward he pushed his soft velvety muzzle into the man's hand and gently nibbled his fingers. Thus friendship was established between them.

And then, for the first time, he noticed a little girl standing just outside. She was a pretty little thing with wavy brown curls that fell in disorder over her merry dancing grey eyes. The face and manner of her dead mother, but the strong will

35

and grey eyes that she had inherited from her father and ancestors of years gone by.

"Come along, Mary, and make friends with the new horse," he cried. "He is very gentle and quiet."

And it was with a curious sensation that Paddy stood still while he felt the small brown hand patting his silky coat. Then he whinnied softly.

"Father!" gasped the child in joyful amazement. "I believe he really loves me."

And a smile dwelt on the Major's face as he replied, "Perhaps so," as they left the stable.

# CHAPTER XIII: *THE OPENING MEET*

If your horse be well fed and in blooming condition,
Both up to the country and up to your weight,
Oh, then give the reins to your youthful ambition,
Sit down in your saddle and keep his head straight!

FROM "HUNTING SONGS."

BUT, in spite of all, Paddy got as fond of little Mary as any dumb creature can love a human; and as for Mary, well, she worshipped and adored him.

And then arose the important question of giving him a name. Mary declared that he must have a new one and boiled up with indignation when her father one day absent-mindedly suggested Neddy.

"Why," she cried hotly, "you would think he was a low-down grey donkey."

And her father, with an amused shrug of his shoulders, resigned the naming to her. And so she arranged it according to her own very vivid imagination. She pictured her father "leading the van" on that gallant grey. Then one evening over the fire she exclaimed:

"Dad, I've got it! Why not Tally Ho?"

And she stuck bravely to that name although her father once nearly broke her limit of patience by enquiring with mock innocence when the christening was to take place. But she got her own way, as she usually did, and Paddy ended up by responding to the name of Tally Ho.

Now a word about his stable-companions. The great bay was called Rajah. A good heavyweight, though not up to much speed. There was also Duchess, another hunter, and an old polo pony.

The opening meet came round rapidly and Tally Ho turned out more satiny and shiny than ever. He stepped out and arched his lovely neck while his dapple coat glistened from very brightness. No one would have dreamed that he came out of a drove of mountain ponies, for only one in a hundred turns out a trump card.

The groom rode him to the meet and his master mounted him on arriving there. The moment he felt his leg across him Tally Ho knew that here was a man who would get his own way, a man who could ride. His firm grip and light hands told the tale.

Hounds moved off to covert. The field followed in a long line of bobbing top hats and pink coats. Mary was riding the dog-quiet old polo pony, who looked very bored.

The fox got away very soon, and the grey found himself in the centre of a good hunting scrum. A gentleman on a fat bay cob led the way through a hole in the hedge and the rest of the field followed. Once away, the going was not difficult. They scurried across a field of stubble and got out at the corner by a lucky gap. Then came the trial. While issuing from a small wood, the Major and his steed were confronted by a high thorny hedge. There was only a few yards run at it, the take-off was sticky and uncertain, it was touch and go whether there was a gaping ditch on the other side, and the Major was on a horse he did not know. But none of these thoughts crossed either of their minds. The rider had ridden worse horses over worse places, and get to hounds he would and could. The horse was full of himself

38

and his abilities, if he had had a weakling on his back who sat still and feebly flapped his reins about—but now . . .

Tally Ho felt himself turned sharp round and he faced the dreaded obstacle. He cantered up to it as hard as the close surroundings would allow. If he wished to clear anything on the off side he must take his chance at the blind fence. As he approached it he caught sight of some brown muddy water beyond. For the first time the horse felt his stout heart quail, but his master was urging him on, with a light feel of the reins on his extended neck. He paused on the brink, collected himself and jumped.

\*　　\*　　\*　　\*　　\*

The fence was cleared and they were both safely away again, but as the Major looked back on the high thorny hedge and the jagged broken banks of the stream—for stream it was—he leaned forward and patted the gallant youngster's shoulder. That was all. It was understood.

But the horse was not without his fun that day. During a check, when everyone was jammed together in a lane, he stretched his head forward and—I fear to say—pulled a fellow horse's tail. He hastily got out of the way, but the horse gave a great buck and the rather red-faced middle-aged dame who sat on his back glided gracefully to the ground. Then our wicked friend gave a jolly horse laugh and thought it a very funny joke.

The field knocked off about four o'clock. The farmer had seen Tally Ho out and felt proud that it was he to whom most of the credit was due.

It was a very long hack back, as hounds had run away from home, and the moon came out long ere the cosy manor was reached. As the Major, who had got off to relieve his horse,

39

trudged silently along through the mud with the reins hanging carelessly over his arm, a verse ran through his mind and made him smile. It ran thus:

> But the longest lane must turn
> And the longest day must end
> And the stable lantern burn
> And the friendly roofs befriend,
> And who that would not ride,
> And who that would not roam,
> For a lodge gate open wide,
> On the long hack home.

This he realised even more the next minute when it began to rain. Then his thoughts ran to Mary, and he wondered how she had got home, and whether she was very anxious about him.

As for his horse, he slouched along with his drooping head in a dreamy sort of way. Twice he stumbled over a root and nearly came down. Perhaps he was thinking of his wild bog home, and wondering how the stallion and all the others were getting on. Who knows?

# CHAPTER XIV: *ANOTHER HUNT AND WHAT CAME OF IT*

A sou'westerly wind and a cloudy sky.

ABOUT a month later a telegram reached the manor. It said:

"Smithfield, Esq. Harkfold Manor.
Good meet on the 14th. Very promising. Come quick and bring one horse and kit for the night.
Leslie Hamilton."

And accordingly the Major took a fond leave of his little daughter and went.

Leslie Hamilton had been under him in the war. A cheery boy, who held his life at no more risk than his pocket-knife. It was not the first time that the master of Harkfold Manor had received a hurried note from Leslie demanding immediate attention. He lived over the other side of the county and was what is termed a "thruster" to hounds.

There was some discussion about which horse was to go. The grey mare, Duchess, was certainly faster, but she could not be compared with the youngster for jumping.

And so that is why one frosty morn Tally Ho found himself on the way to a meet with his master, accompanied by Leslie, on an aged black racehorse.

It was a lovely day. The sun rose over the bare waving tree-tops with a red glow of warmth. The birds twittered gaily and the dry crackling leaves made a pleasant rustle under their feet. The Major, conscious of being attired in a new pink coat, whistled too.

The meet was not a popular one, at least not to the swells who come out only to show off their clothes to their friends; but, as Leslie truly remarked, it was a "likely draw."

The huntsman lost no time in cheering hounds into covert, and soon the swelling chorus told that they were on a line. First Harmony gave a whimper, then Neptune and Diana caught it up, followed by Harlequin, until the whole pack were hot on a breast-high scent. They streamed away over a ploughed field, and so silently did they work that most of the field on the far side of the covert were totally unconscious of the proceedings. Luckily, however, the Major and his friend saw them in time and set off at full speed to catch them up.

The run lasted for fully four miles without stop or stay. Then hounds made a cast. But they were off again in no time, hardly before the blown horses of the five remaining had caught up.

In about twenty more minutes the field had dwindled to three. The Major, Leslie, and the huntsman still survived, and the latter's horse was certainly nearly dead beat. Then even these came to a standstill, for right in front of them the way was blocked by a wide muddy brook. It was full ten feet across and quite that in depth. The huntsman went at it with a will, and if hearts could have thrown him across he would have been well landed. But it was not so. The horse hardly lifted his legs off the ground, and tumbled in with a splash. They were both carried downstream where they landed safely by the ford.

But now to the Major. Nothing daunted he gave Tally Ho his head, urged him into a gallop and came at it with

FLOUNDERED UP THE STEEP SLIPPERY BANK

great energy. The horse sprung up with all the strength of his powerful quarters beneath him, landed with his forelegs on the far side and his hindlegs in the water. After a violent struggle he floundered up the steep slippery bank, and as the Major looked back he saw Leslie take a great leap and land safely. He let out a cheer, but, alas, the old black had had too much galloping for his advanced years, and suddenly crumpled up, stumbled, pecked, and fell.

"Go on," yelled poor Leslie while yet in mid-air, and the Major turned and went on.

The hounds came to a standstill soon after as the fox had gone to ground, and it was with no little pride that Major Smithfield rode home in the dark after handing over the tired pack to a much bedraggled huntsman.

All this was told fluently, if slightly exaggerated in Leslie's epistle to Mary—for he had a great liking for that little person—and his praises of the young horse were innumerable. So Mary made up her naughty little mind to have a hunt on this wonderful Tally Ho.

Now she would not have thought of this had she not known that the horse was peculiarly attached to her. Did she not also know that he would take tit-bits out of no one's hand but hers, and that no one else would he suffer to ride him bareback? But anyhow he liked her, she liked him. That decided it.

This accounted for one morning when her father stood on the lee side of a covert talking to a friend. He was mounted on Rajah, the bay, as the grey horse had been left at home. What was his surprise, then, to suddenly perceive, like an apparition, a small muddy figure, hatless, with torn clothes, whom he barely recognised to be his daughter. Not only that, but she was mounted on the said grey, who was placidly jogging along, with an old sack for a saddle and an old blinkered harness-bridle which did not show off to advantage the handsome head of her mount. Before her shocked parent could get in a word she cried breathlessly:

"Oh! Hello, Dad! Here you are. We lost our way and I fell off into a ditch, and Tally stood still and——"

"Mary," demanded her father somewhat sternly, "what is the meaning of this turn-out?"

"That—er—well, you see, I couldn't find the other stuff and we were in a hurry and, as I was saying, Tally stood still and——"

"We can talk that over at home, Mary. Now will you please go back and change? Give the horse over to Atly."

"I am very sorry, Dad," answered his daughter penitently, "but I *did* so want a ride on him," and she turned away.

"Excuse her, she's still very young," said her father, turning to the gentleman beside him.

"All the more wonder," was the smiling answer. "But wait! One more word. I think that that horse of yours is worth his weight in gold."

And the Major, in spite of himself, agreed.

# CHAPTER XV: *A POINT-TO-POINT MEETING*

Silence—then from the crowds a hum
Deep and expectant—"Here they come!"
"Who's that leading?" and "Still the brown!"
"Now for the double!" and "Two of 'em down!"

FROM "SCATTERED SCARLET."

TALLY HO lived for a long time in this happy place. He was now coming seven and therefore nearly in the prime of his life. During this time he grew very attached to the inmates of the old manor. Morning after morning he would wait longingly to hear the long stride of his master and the smaller tread of his young mistress coming down the yard on their early visit.

He had hunted a lot and had always jumped with fearlessness and caution. Sometimes he was inclined to be a trifle hot and pull, but as old Atly exclaimed one day when he had been keener than ever, "Why an' what would be the use of the creather if he didn't remind one he was of wild blood betimes? I ask ye that now!"

And no one stood up to answer him.

The racing season was drawing near and Major Smithfield had entered him for several small point-to-point races. He was fed up into hard condition and sometimes was taken for trial gallops.

Here he was in his element. There were no nasty gaps or trappy scrambles to check at, only good open fences and wide unbroken heath. On these occasions his master gave

45

him his head, and though jumping was really more in his line than galloping, he could set a fair pace for a few miles.

He remembered one particular afternoon when the sun was setting over the distant misty hills—one of those quiet afternoons when even the birds seem silent. The glowing sun sent a strange ruddy light around, and as he galloped forward he imagined that he was leaving all care and sorrow behind him; that the world was just a long plain, never ending; that he was the only living thing in it, and that he was free. Then he felt a touch on the rein, heard his master talking to him, and he returned to everyday life again.

At last the day of his first point-to-point arrived. It was merely a small meeting, and he was entered for a three-mile race. The weather was fine, and Atly rode him round with a big cloth marked 13 on his side. "Unlucky," thought the Major, not that he minded, but the Irish are a naturally superstitious race and might—well, anyhow, he hoped for the best!

It was indeed enough to make any horse nervous; the gay clothes and waving flags and the noise were—well—terrible! So thought our friend as he was led round the ring before starting. The bookies were each trying to outvie their rivals; the shouts of "Two to one, bar one; two to one, bar one", "Five to one on Black Prince", "Come to the good old firm", and so on, augmented the din, while sometimes he heard his own name when there was a momentary silence. The odds were against him twenty-three to one, but what else could you expect of a such-like youngster?

Also, some tinkers* wandered about with ironware to sell. Some very disreputable old women pestered the cars with their "Race cad, Lidy; race cad. Plaise buy one, ar'm a poor

* Gipsies.

46

ole woman with ten children. Race cad. Och ye," as her
ware was declined, "may the saints shower curses upon ye";
and some rather drunken men rolled about shouting and
singing, for the society of an inferior Irish race meeting is by
no means picked.

The Major rode the young horse himself, as he always
said: "What's the use of keeping a horse if you don't get the
fun out of him?" His colours were crimson with bright gold
hoops, and Tally Ho returned the compliment by shying
at him.

Together they cantered to the starting-post. The horse
was so frightened that he started three times before the
word, and when the red flag did come down he bounded
forward as if shot and soon took the lead. He flung two
fences behind him without a mistake, and soon he tackled
the third, a slippery bank with a nasty take-off. But now the
Major suddenly realised that he was out of control. His
speed was not quite as fast as some, but he easily outstripped
everyone at his fences, so now he was full three fields in
front of the rest. But still the galloping had gone to his head
and he was mad to be on.

Unluckily, while rounding a turn, they ran wide of the
flag. The horse would not stop and the rider could not stop,
and so they galloped on for another half-mile when at last
Tally Ho was brought to a standstill by a high brick wall.
His master did not know where they were until he struck a
road that ran past the manor, full fourteen miles from home,
and not knowing the way back to the racecourse he thought
that he would follow it. He was clearly very put out, for he
kept muttering to himself: "Stupid brute! What's the use of
paying for the feed of an obstinate beast like this; nothing in
his silly head but stubbornness! All these handsome creatures!

Give me a good, ugly, decent-minded old animal with some sense in him. I'll sell him straight away when I get home!"

Indeed, he was sorely tempted to call on Farmer O'Hagen as he passed and demand his money back, but he gave up the idea when he remembered that perhaps he was worth his keep as a hunter after all.

As for the object of his thoughts, nothing could have looked more sorry, what with his head down somewhere in the region of his knees, and his soft brown eyes bent guiltily on the ground, he looked as if he really realised his crime.

An owl hooted twice, a bat swooped by on silent wings. The young horse suddenly felt a pat on his neck, and a cheerful voice said: "Well, lad, that's over now. Have you finished inspecting the roots?"

His heart warmed to his master and Tally Ho loved as he had never loved before.

# CHAPTER XVI: *GOOD SERVICE*

Your season's toil is over,
　With grass that sweeps your knees
You search for cool wet clover,
　In friendship with the bees. . . .

No Whip's triumphant halloa,
　No horn's entrancing tune
Has power to bid you follow
　From out these fields of June.
FROM "SCATTERED SCARLET."

THE sun was gaining strength, the trees were already in bloom, and summer was near at hand. A fresh breeze was blowing from the river carrying with it the delicious scent of the lilac, and spring flowers lay scattered on the grass. It was a peaceful scene that presented itself in the old meadow: a cow lay drowsily basking on the ground, Rajah and Duchess were having a languid quarrel on the far side of the field, and Delhi, the old polo pony, who had been having a roll on the soft cool grass, had collapsed on to his side and lay there fast asleep.

The gate opened and our friend came trotting in. He walked up to the pony and gave him a playful dig in the ribs, and having roused him, was spitefully told that runaways were not allowed in that field.

"Neither are crocks," retorted the grey grumpily, and then they both turned their backs on each other; and Tally Ho stalked over to the other two and inquisitively demanded what the quarrel was about.

"Mustn't poke your innocent little nose where it's not wanted," answered Rajah. "If you really want to know we were disagreeing as to whether you are a young fool or not, and I am sure I am right in saying that you are one after that point-to-point affair. That's about all. Satisfied?"

Tally Ho was not, but, to change the subject, meekly suggested that each horse should tell his life-story. This was agreed upon, and they all four gathered under the old elms and started. The grey, who being the youngest told his first, related as already put down in this book. Rajah's story was very long-winded and meant nothing. He had been bought and sold many times, but had never fallen into really bad hands, and at last had been bought by Major Smithfield at a fair.

Duchess, the old white mare, came next. Her story was a sad one. She had been ill and harshly treated, and a long scar from her withers to her saddle-mark told of the accident she had had while straining at a heavy load under a lashing whip. She had run away to her present master and had been kept ever since.

"And now," exclaimed Rajah gleefully, "let's do something else——"

"And my story?" asked Delhi.

"Yours!" was the scornful answer. "Come on, lads, let's bundle old boney to the river and give him a ducking."

"No," said the grey, taking an unexpected lead, "leave him alone and let him tell his story."

Delhi turned to him and just said "Thank you," but in such a way that the young horse felt satisfied. Then the pony started.

"I was born in India. My first remembrance is of lying beside my mother in a warm tent. The walls were covered with velvet hangings and the floor was covered by a rich oriental carpet, for I was the property of a great Maharajah and was considered one of the handsomest horses of the age. I was jet-black, as I am now, and I was trained for polo and kept solely for my master's use. How well I remember my early home. The old courtyard with the fountain in the centre, the lurking shadows, staring sun and the parakeets who flew screaming around. How well I remember outside the gaunt walls of the palace, the massive temple surrounded by the tall palms from which unearthly music would sometimes pour forth.

"But all this ended the day when Major, then Lieutenant, Smithfield came to pay a visit. The Maharajah was proud to have a white man in his palace and gave him many presents, among which was an ivory-wrought chest inlaid with gold, a diamond-hilted sword, and the best horse in the royal stables. That is how I came to live with him.

"For many years I played polo in India, until at last my master—our master—left for England. I accompanied him, of course, and I said farewell for ever to the land where I was born. The English climate did not suit me, and even now I am far more liable to catch cold than any of you who are born and brought up in these polar regions. Well, as I said, I came to England and lived with my master, and even learnt a bit of that queer sport fox-hunting, until the war, and as the Major had got very fond of me, and I fond of him, —who is not?—he decided to take me, if possible. And so on a wet dreary evening I boarded the ship for Calais and went out to the war.

"For four long years I stayed in Flanders, 'stormed at with shot and shell.' Twice I was wounded and once saved my master's life. It was like this. One evening, after a very long

51

march over a bare country of burning homes and fallen
ashes, we were rounding a dangerous corner. I stepped on a
fallen log and stumbled badly, such as to throw my master
on to my neck. A second after a bullet whizzed by just where
his head had been. Thus unconsciously I saved his life and
he has vowed never to sell me. I have lived with him nearly
all my life and I only wish to die in his service. That's my
story."

There was a long silence. The sun was setting and the
shadows crept eastward. The other horses stood as if en-
chanted, and Delhi waited for their answer; and as the twilight darkened they saw his fine old head silhouetted against
the sky, and one and all realised that his had been no idle
boast of his looks. At last Rajah spoke.

"I am very sorry—we all are—don't mind me—I didn't
know," he said brokenly.

"We made a great mistake," said Tally Ho.

"Thank you again," said the old polo pony.

# CHAPTER XVII: *THE WICKLOW SHOW AND AFTER*

"Showing" is an art in itself.
And a failure is not a sin,
For a sportsman knows, in the midst of his woes,
That everybody can't win.

THE summer days fled past, the monotony only broken by the Wicklow Show. Tally Ho never could be induced to jump in cold blood, for, having once hunted, like a true hunter he thought it poor sport indeed. Anyhow, Major Smithfield had entered him and Duchess for the hunter class, and he thought that perhaps the grey would jump when in among other horses. If he didn't there was no harm done, and so that is how the Mayo gelding came to try his luck in the show ring.

It was a fine warm day and everyone was decked out in their gayest of colours. This, however, did not worry him much as he had got used to crowds by this time. We will not say much about the class, let it suffice to say that he went in *without* and came out of the show ring *with* a red rosette on his noseband. Everyone clapped, which rather upset him, but he had a greater trial still in front of him.

Before the Novice Jumping Competition he was taken round to look at the fences. His number was 42, and number 41 set a bad example by knocking all the fences down. When his turn came at last he rushed the first hurdle at a great speed. The next was a bank and he got over this well.

The people clapped, the horse reared, and Major John Smithfield's hat rolled into the ditch. This made matters worse as everyone laughed and the noise thoroughly upset the grey, who ran out at the stone wall and knocked a wing down. His master got him by the head and put him at it again, determined to get him over. Tally Ho was now equally determined to stay where he was, his fright having changed to a surly stubbornness. For a few minutes it was a battle between horse and man, and the spectators leaned forward tensely to see who would win. In the excitement of the moment the judges forgot to dismiss them from the field for having refused three times, and there was a dead silence. At last Tally Ho gave himself a final heave round, threw up his heels and galloped through the gate in spite of curb and rein.

The horse had won.

*    *    *    *    *

The cubbing came and went and the season settled in in real earnest. The horses each went out roughly twice a fortnight and in between were exercised daily by Atly. A new pony had been bought for Mary, called Stumpy. Indeed, he seemed stumpy all over, for he was about $12\frac{1}{2}$ hands, and pure white except for one black ear, and his muzzle was very short. Stumpy seemed to have taken the place of old Delhi, for the latter hardly ever went out hunting now, and most of his days were spent in a large roomy cowshed on a bed of tan. There was plenty of room for him to trot up and down and he would have liked it very much only he missed the company.

Tally Ho was nearly aged now and he was beginning to turn out a promising hunter. He had been in several good runs and had once got his master the brush.

54

It was about this time that the frost set in. One morning when Mary got up the ground outside was white and the icicles clung to the window-ledge. "No hunting this morning, Mary," said her father, when she came down to breakfast; and he was right. Not only that morning but the morning after, and the morning after that, was there no hunting. Day after day did Mary rise hopefully, but, catching sight of the frost-blurred window, would sink back into bed with a sigh. Then came the snow.

Soon after this the grey developed that bad trick of wind-sucking. At first he did it to amuse himself, then it became a habit, until he awoke one morning with, oh, such a pain! He remained lying down until someone came into his box. Someone else said, "He has colic, send for the vet.," and then he was left alone. It was unlucky that Atly had gone to town for a few days and the Major was laid up with 'flu. An inexperienced lad was left in charge of the stables that day until Atly came home in the evening. The vet. came at last and the horse had a bit put in his mouth so that he could not shut it. Then some horrid medicine was poured down his throat, and the vet. left orders that he was to have another dose at three o'clock and went away.

About three the Major, feeling better, thought he would take a stroll, and on passing the stables he heard a great deal of talk going on in one of the boxes. He went into the yard and looked into the grey's box. What a sight met his eyes! The inexperienced lad was standing on a chair, with his shirt-sleeves rolled up and holding a medicine bottle in one hand and a small medicine glass in the other. The unfortunate grey was backed into a corner, the gardener hung on to his forelock, and the chauffeur stood pulling his ears about, while littered about the box stood four or five workmen who had dropped in on their way from the village to "see the fun"!

On being asked the reason for this, the undaunted chorus that greeted the Major was something like this:

"Aye, yer honer, 'twas loike this——" "Listen, now and I am telling ye——" "Faix, 'twas grand sport——" "Hie, ye let oi get a word in——" "Saints protect us——" "He nearly knocked the ligs from under me that hoss did——" "I am kilt, oi am——" and so on.

All the rest were dismissed and the master took the boy in charge aside. I will not say what he told him, but it's true that when he let that inexperienced lad go, that lad felt more inexperienced than ever.

As for Tally Ho, he had no more medicine, because it had already been spilt on the ground; and the next morning never was there a fitter horse that awoke to hear that the frost had thawed.

# CHAPTER XVIII: *THE ACCIDENT*

> Fast flies the fox away—faster
>     The hounds from the covert are freed,
>   The horn to the mouth of the Master,
>     The spur to the flank of his steed.
>
> FROM "HUNTING SONGS."

ALL traces of frost had disappeared and the sun again reigned over all. The trees joyfully waved their thin swaying arms, as if glad to be rid of their heavy loads of snow, and the ground, though still hard, had been greatly softened by rain.

Though fairly fit, the grey was not well enough to go out hunting. Rajah had a very bad cough, and Duchess's fetlocks were swelled like puff-balls, the effects of underwork and standing all day in the stable. It was obvious that the Major could *not* ride Stumpy, and as he was very keen to get to that particular meet, what remained but Delhi?

Yes, Delhi should go! Stumpy was too fresh for Mary to ride and he even kicked Atly off in the yard, and so back to the stable he went, and Delhi was groomed and brushed until his coat shone and you could see your face in his saddlery.

All the horses looked out and said "Good-bye" and "Good luck" to him as he was led through the yard, and it was almost pathetic to see the airs he put on as he strode out of the gate to the front door.

His master in his new pink coat mounted him and they started off at a brisk trot down the drive. The meet was at a

57

place called "Seven Oaks," four miles away, and why the Major had wanted so much to go was because an old friend of his was coming there also. "Perhaps it is best that I took Delhi with me," he mused; "anyhow, come on!"

The meet was a smart one and it took him quite a time to find his friend. This was a very dark man, evidently foreign, dressed in badly cut European clothes. He stood by a big smart car, with a chauffeur sitting in it, and was looking around him with an air of calm bewilderment. The Major rode up to him and shook hands.

"Ah, here is our friend the Maharajah," he said. "You do not know me? Young Lieutenant Smithfield, riding the best horse in the royal stables?"

An exclamation of surprise and pleasure broke through the other man's lips. "Strange," he said in a slightly foreign accent, "strange to meet you here. You Englishmen are wonderful, always the same. You have still got the horse?"

"Yes, we stick together like glue it seems."

After this the two men launched into conversation and were only interrupted by the hounds moving off. Indeed, if it had not been for Delhi's violent prancings, they would have gone off out of sight.

"He takes kindly to it," murmured the Maharajah softly to himself, as the horse and man rode off. "And who's to blame him? Ah, my lovely Dhoophal,* thou art happy."

Hounds got away very soon and Delhi was not last in the van. They hurried over a grass field, scurried down a lane, rushed through a gap, and at the end of a field of plough jumped a wide gaping ditch into a grass ride. This was strewn with fallen leaves and dead bracken, and as the pony cantered along his old heart sang with the joy of being alive

* Red Sunlight.

CAME OUT WITH A RED ROSETTE

and it gave him new strength. As they emerged from this ride everyone crammed at a fence on the right side. It was a horrid thing, an old stone stile overgrown with ivy and brambles, and many horses refused or ran out at it. But Delhi knew no hesitation. He went at it splendidly and rose like a stag. . . .

The hunt swept on like a mighty wave, leaving two horses fallen. One was running round the field and its rider was rising from a ditch on the far side of the stile, very wet and muddy; the other horse lay struggling on the ground with his rider beneath him. It was Delhi!

    \*     \*     \*     \*     \*

That night a smart car drove up to the Manor. It was the Maharajah bringing home his friend who had broken his hip.

Later on the distant sound of a gun was heard, and little did the other horses know how soon his wish had come true —old Delhi was at rest.

    \*     \*     \*     \*     \*

"The horses are to be sold." That was the sentence that passed through Atly's lips the morning after the accident when he entered the stable. Only he realised what this really meant; only *he* had made all the arrangements for the following morning, for, though the Major would in time get strong again, it was no earthly use for the horses to be eating their heads off in the stables, better even to get rid of them than that.

Rajah was going to a rich gentleman in the neighbourhood for 235 guineas. Duchess was to be sent up to be sold with Tally Ho. Stumpy was being put out to grass to "rough it."

The Major was going to a nursing-home, and little Mary for the present was going to stay with an elderly aunt.

The last morning at Harkfold Manor was not a happy one. Mary came down to say "Good-bye" to the horses and shed tears over each of them, but when she came to her favourite she broke down completely and sobbed out all her woes on his mane. He poked his nose gently and enquiringly into her small hand, ate the bit of sugar he found there with great satisfaction, and for the second time in his life the grey wondered what all the fuss was about.

Then Atly came to say that "Missy" had better go now as it was time to start. It seemed queer that Atly should be so affected at parting with the grey. Had not the old groom passed thousands of young horses through his hands without the quiver of an eyelid? And now, when he saddled this horse for the last time and led him through the well-known yard and under the old ivy-grown arch, his heart seemed to burst with sorrow.

When they arrived at the station Atly said farewell to the two horses, for he had to return and care for the house in the absence of his master. The two were in their boxes, the guard gave the signal, and the train moved out of the station.

Thus Harkfold Manor fled like a happy vision out of Tally Ho's life and left him alone and shivering in the uncomfortable box, while the train puffed on to its destination.

# CHAPTER XIX: *HUNTING*

How his throbbing heart beat
As on swift little feet
He crept stealthily down by the wall
While a man on a grey
With a loud "Gone away"
Gave the line of his flight to them all.

FROM "SCATTERED SCARLET."

"SOLD!" The auctioneer's hammer fell with a crash, and on looking round the dingy yard and turned-up, expectant faces, Tally Ho saw his new master step forward. He was a youngish man, tall, slight, and fair, with high cheekbones and a deep low voice. Although obviously not a gentleman he was distinctly good-looking. Jim Sanders, second Whip to the —— hounds, was a good chap in his way though he inherited that fault of most of his calling, paying too much attention to the hounds and not enough to his horses. Still, Jim meant to behave well to them, though sometimes he did give them a clout when in a "flurry," and so when he stepped up to the platform, took over his new mount, and said in a soft Irish brogue "Now come now, you! We'll be afther havin' grand runs you and oi. What, hey? Come on now. Thank ye, hey!" the grey did not think he was badly off.

When they both at last arrived at the kennels the horse was very tired and just went to sleep without wondering what his abode was like. He had not seen old Duchess before he left, but he hoped that she had got a good home for her sake.

The following morning he found that he was in a long row of stalls with eight or nine horses in them belonging to the hunt. That day was a non-hunting one, but the next day Tally Ho was saddled and the Whip mounted and rode to the meet with the hounds. The horse thought these very dull stupid things and kicked one, but after this received such a smack that made his ear tingle painfully all through the day.

On arrival at the meet, a very smart gentleman hailed the Whip.

"Good morning, Jim, that's a new horse you have there?"

Jim touched his hat respectfully. "Shure, yer honer. A grand un, what, hey?"

"Yes, Jim, you have made a good buy there."

Then they went on to covert. While Tally Ho was waiting half asleep on one side a little red animal stole out of the bushes and made for the open country. Suddenly the whole covert seemed alive with sounds. "Grr away, garn away, garn awa-y," yelled Jim. "Tally 'o, Tally 'o," came from the other side of the wood, and Tally Ho started at his own name. The next moment he felt the spurs at his side and he needed no second bidding. Away he flew like lightning; the wind sang in his ears. Jim stood up in his stirrups. "Garn away, Charley, garn aw-a-y!" he shouted, and the covert seemed to echo his words. "Garn aw-a-y," it answered.

Now the rest of the field were pouring in from all sides, but the horse and rider passed unmolested as the cry "'Ware Whip" went down the line. A fence rose in front—it was gone; a field—a wood—a stream—another wood—more fields—all fled like a vision through the grey's mind. Here a gate—there a ride—a great fence covered with flags, red ones. " 'Ware wire," yells someone, but too late—over—sound landing—plough—fields again.

\* \* \* \* \*

"Well done, Billy," said Jim, patting him. "There be few horses who would have done that! What! Hey?"

Tally Ho, for the first time since the run started, looked around him well. He was standing in a circle composed of about five persons. In the centre the tired hounds were baying and leaping round the Master who was "breaking up" the fox. What of the gallant party who had been at the meet?

A gentleman rode up—the same who had spoken to the Whip before.

"Well, Jim, the best run of the season, I think, though few here to witness it," looking round the scant company. "Well, man, never mind, 'handsome is as handsome does,' that's my motto. But I say, Jim, that grey there seems to possess both qualities; but can't he go though! Why, Jim, you ought to race him."

"Aye, yer honer, win the hunt races. What, hey?"

"But, man alive! joking apart, I should have a dashed good try."

"That I will. But shure ole Billy would be there, all nice like. Off they goes. There's Billy who would be afther wonderin' and standin' there the while. What, hey?"

"Look here, Jim, honestly. I like the horse, but as he is not for sale I would like to race him. Bet he could go! Listen, I pay all expenses, entries and damages; you will have full privilege to grumble and grouse over him all day long if you like. Now, Jim, be a good fellow. Do you agree?"

"To be shure, yer honer, I do."

"Good chap. Well, bye-bye, Jim."

"Good evening, yer honer."

But as Jim was riding home he slapped the grey on the shoulder and said: "Faix, Bill! wot a chance, lad! Saints alive! Why, I'll be a rich man before long. Shure an' ar will. What, hey?"

But "Bill" only heard a low mumble, and did not understand. He only thought what a low common voice the man had got, and wished himself back with the others at Harkfold Manor.

# CHAPTER XX: *COME ON*

A word in season, the wave of the hand,
  To show the flag at the turn of the land.
A sudden rustle and restless tread—
  "Off!" and the first fence looms ahead.

FROM "SCATTERED SCARLET."

DAY after day passed. Tally Ho was one of the best horses in the hunt stables; well known about the country for his wonderful jumping and good manners. Day after day he would hear that wonderful "Tally Ho—Garn away—Whoop along there," and then came the horn and he would tremble with joy as the sound thrilled him through and through; and next moment he would receive a clout on the head and a few harsh words and off he would clatter, down the ride. And yet he loved this life, too. His heart was with the hounds, and that bold heart never failed him though he was ready at times to drop from exhaustion. So much so that he was nicknamed "Bould heart" by the countryfolk around.

But the season came to an end and the racing started. The gentleman in the pink coat, Mr. Jameson by name, had now got the grey for the time being at his house. It was in a way hard on Tally Ho—for his gallant work all through the winter had worn him out no little—to have his work over only to find a harder path in front of him. He had already run in two races, and had on one occasion received second prize. Mr. Jameson was a good rider, barring rather heavy

hands, and was very keen to have him entered for the Hunt
Steeplechase. This was done and on the 4th of April the
grey hunter found himself in the big ring before the start.

There were twelve others entered for the race, including
some well-known steeplechasers called Trophy, Connemara
Lassie, Billy Boy, and Chang. Connemara Lassie and the great
mouse-coloured horse called Chang had been racing for over
nine years. What chance for a horse like Tally Ho, however
good a hunter, for good hunters don't always make good
racehorses!

The race was a four-mile one, the going was very heavy,
and the distance far. No chance for the 10 to 1 grey.

Anyhow, from the start he took the lead, to everyone's
surprise. On he went in grand style, leaving Chang in the far
rear. Now they were lost to view, now seen again, the light
dapple-grey always leading. "He's down, ar tell yer." "He's
not, he's g'wen now—grand." "Here they come." "Aye,
come HUP!" "Saints protect us, he's down." "He is not."
Thus spake the spectators as the horses passed the grand-
stand for the first time. Alas, now the good grey showed
signs of flagging! The pace had been too hard for him—
CRASH!!—down came horse and rider; the grey lay on the
ground.

The Field passed safely over him, and then, lo and be-
hold! the dead rose again and in no time the grey and his
rider were off once more. The attention of the spectators
was now turned on to Connemara Lassie who had taken the
lead. Chang was close behind her, and Trophy had just
fallen, knocking Billy Boy down with her. Billy Boy rose
again without his rider, who lay grovelling in the mud, and
continued the race. Trophy lay still. Meanwhile a grey horse
was advancing steadily. He, on recovery, had been three

fields behind; the distance had been lessened to two, now to one. One field behind the leader!

The winning-post was in view; the last fence was cleared; the Connemara mare had dropped behind and Chang had taken the lead. Suddenly a grey horse burst through the rest, his flanks covered with white foam and mud splashes all around. The frantic rider had lost his hat and whip, and was now digging his spurs into his horse's heaving sides. Then the crowd realised that this outsider was going to stand for a place—for a win. Faster—stride by stride he caught up with Chang—passed him. And the winning-post stood within three lengths.

Now the crowd burst into a wild frenzy, cheered, waved, shouted, did anything, in fact, on the spur of the moment. A certain Farmer O'Hagen seized a fat dame by the waist in his joy and imprinted a kiss on her cheek. A certain second Whip clapped a bookie so hard on the back that he knocked him down off his stand. A certain . . . But to return.

To Tally Ho it seemed nothing at all. He was near dead beat, no one knew that better than he did, but he distinguished one voice from the rest. It said only:

"Come on, lad. Come on!"

The voice came from a pale, weak-looking man in a bath-chair and Tally Ho knew it. True instinct told him that it came from the only man he had really loved. "Come on!" He—Tally Ho—must do something greater, greater than this. The riderless Billy Boy was just in front, and the grey extended once more, with all his remaining strength, and passed him—the winning-post sped by. Then the exhausted animal did a thing which few 'chasers have ever done—collapsed on to his side and lay there. . . .

The hum around him rose and fell, he knew nothing

except that he imagined a voice he knew well coming out of the blur, saying, "Well done, laddie. Well done!"

And he fell back with a sigh of content and all was darkness.

*    *     *     *     *

He awoke to hear the drone of voices, and as they became more distinct he looked around and found himself in his own box.

"Can't I do anything?" said the voice of Mr. Jameson.

"Is it his wind?" said that of Jim.

"Yes, gentlemen," said a strange voice. "Quite gone in the wind, I'm afraid. No more hunting or racing for him."

"Can't I do anything?" muttered Jameson again.

"Well, sir," said the other, "if you want to kill him—yes."

"No, no, I mean, can't I do anything to help him?"

"Not much beyond good care and a small amount of work. If I were you, gentlemen, I should sell him."

There was a silence.

"Would a livery stable do?" asked Jim.

"Um," said the strange voice which Tally Ho now recognised as that of the vet. "Um, well—er—ye-s."

"Shure, ye don't seem plaised about it," said Jim.

"Yes. It will do," said the vet. shortly. "Gentlemen, good evening."

And they all filed out into the cold dark night, leaving the grey alone to doze in comfort.

# CHAPTER XXI: *THE BATTERED BRIGADE*

The mark of a stake in the shoulder,
The brand of a wall on the knee,
Are scars to the careless beholder,
And blemishes, so it may be;
But every such blemish endorses
The pluck of a steed unafraid,
And the heart of a lover of horses
Goes out to the Battered Brigade.

FROM "SCATTERED SCARLET."

"THE Battered Brigade"; and the noble grey hunter who had made his name far and wide was now one of them! Hard it was that now he was to be repaid for all his great services by being sold, and to a livery stables at that. But Jim Sanders had the cup on his table and the forty pounds in his pocket, and the thought never entered his mind. The horse certainly was a "blower," and his "confounded concert," as Jim expressed it, would make him an object of laughter, besides the obvious fact that he would be left behind. If only Tally Ho could have known that it made no odds whether he passed Billy Boy or not, as the latter had no rider. If only he could have known that his former master's "Come on" was merely an admiring expression. If only he could have known that that last effort was his undoing. . . .

But Tally Ho never knew all this, so what's the point of dwelling on it? He only vaguely wondered as he rattled along in the train to Dublin—which was to be his future home—

69

he only vaguely wondered if he were going to a race or show, and did not understand why everyone laughed at the notice painted over his door. It said, "BILLY. DANGEROUS," and someone had chalked it up there for a joke.

The train paused, jolted, and came to a standstill with a jerk that nearly threw "Billy" off his legs. It was dark now, and when he was led, stiff and weary, out of his box into a narrow cobbled street, he did not notice the dark grimy houses on each side or the murky, heavy air which blew gently from the river. He did not see, when he was led under a dusty, low arch, the sign that said:

DUBLIN LIVERY STABLES

Horses for Hire Daily at Reduced Charges.

E. Fink & Son.

He only knew that he was now in a box, that a rug was thrown over him, that he was desperately sleepy. . . .

Morning—sunlight—straw! That was his first impression of the Dublin Livery Stables. Morning it was, for the sunlight was filtering through a crack in the wall, and he was lying on straw—dirty old straw it was true, but still, straw. His box was narrow and none of the cleanest; the top half of the door was ajar and he pushed it open with his muzzle. A bony, filthy little cob whinnied to him from the yard where he was harnessed to a rubbish cart. Tally Ho turned away in disgust. What business had he, dirty little democrat that he was, to whinny to Tally Ho, the well-known hunter, winner of the hunt cup and so on! And yet the grey would never have believed that six months from now he would ask advice from the little bay cob in the dust cart.

Later on a groom brought him a feed and gave him a good

grooming. "Mike," the groom, certainly was an Irishman, as having been nipped in the fleshy part of his calf by the grey, he threw a dandy-brush at him and exclaimed: "Och ye! yer clean enough now, ye filthy-lookin' bhrute ye."

At about ten o'clock Tally Ho was saddled and led out. An elderly lady was waiting in a brown habit, and on her nervous enquiries as to her new mount's age, she was told that he was seventeen years old and "safe as a house." His name was Dapple so she was told, and she insisted on calling him either Dapple Girl or Grey Lady, for she would not believe that he was a gelding.

It felt queer to the fine horse to be trotting out of the arch with someone quite strange on his back. Beyond the fact that he was in a strange town and carrying a strange saddle which made his charge—for charge, indeed, she was, considering she did not even know how to hold her reins—sit all sideways (this was a side-saddle). She was no fine rider, this brown bundle, and bumped about so that it was all the grey could do to refrain from kicking her off.

After a very short dull ride along the road and back he was taken in. The next day the same thing happened and then he was left in for three days and taken out again. This time, as soon as they got on to a green patch of grass, his feet began to tickle and itch to be away. In his heart his remarks must have been a little like this: "Stupid woman, can't she ride?" Silence. "No, I don't think she can!" Another painful silence. "I have decided she can't." "Why will she chuck my mouth so? Bother her. She makes my back ache, bumping up and down like that! Silly woman!" Certainly the more he tried to pretend that nothing was the matter, the more he realised that something was wrong. When at last they came to the gate entering the great park he could bear that itch no

71

longer, and with a happy buck and bound was away across the sound green turf. He was not to be blamed—any horse would have done it. Leave your own in for three days, getting plenty of corn, then take him out, put a bad rider on him and see what will happen. But how Tally Ho loved that gallop! The bundle fell off at the first hint of a kick, and the only thing that marred the horse's joy was that hounds were not in front of him. But he had a great time all the same.

In the evening a riderless horse was led home by a boy to the stables. A grey horse who looked black because of his coat of mud; a horse whose reins were broken in half and a horse whose saddle clung under his belly. Altogether a disreputable horse. He was roughly thrown into his box and left there.

Late that evening the master, Mr. Fink, came down. He was a tall, dark, cruel man and was in an awful temper.

"Lost one o' me best customers," he bellowed. "Beat the beast, beat 'im. Beat 'im till 'e squeals for mercy."

Tally Ho was taken out and beaten, beaten with a long-lashed driving whip, but he never squealed! And when he was thrown bleeding, breathless, angry, and miserable into his dirty little box his temper was ruined.

The Tally Ho that night was a different horse from the Tally Ho he had been that morning.

# CHAPTER XXII: *THE LAST HUNT*

When the music begins and a right one's away,
When hoof-strokes are thudding like drums on the ground,
  The old spirit wakes in the worn-looking grey
And the pride of his youth comes to life at a bound. . . .

To the best of us all comes a day and a day
  When the pace of the leaders shall leave us forlorn,
So we'll give him a cheer—the old galloping grey—
  As he labours along to the lure of the horn.
FROM "SCATTERED SCARLET."

NOT that Mr. Fink was really such a bad man, but he had an awful temper and when thoroughly roused nothing short of cruelty would satisfy him. True it was that the brown bundle never returned again to the Dublin Livery Stables; true also that the grey was laid up for a week in his box with the "most h'awful temper a man can imagine," but what of that? Whenever anyone entered his box he laid back his ears, bared his teeth and kicked. Who was to blame for that?

One day, however, about six weeks after this episode, a young man of about twenty came into the yard.

"Hie ye," he called to a groom, "com' here now and tell me 'ow many gees ye got here."

"Well, yer honer, I would be afther thinkin'——"

"Don't think—say."

"We-l-l, sixtin."

"Right now, I wants two t'morrow."

"Yes, yer honer, wot for?"

"Huntin' ye . . . you. Wot else? Gimme a grey and a brown."

"Shure yer honer," answered the groom, scratching his woolly head. "How far be the meet?"

" 'Black Bull,' twelve, fourtin, fiftin, twent . . .' "

"And will ye be afther takin' the horses all that way?"

"No, it's ten mile. Have 'em ready at eleven t'morrow."

"That I will."

Thus the young man swaggered out of the yard, leaving the puzzled groom staring after him.

"Faix now, think o' that," he murmured. "Why, Dapple an' Puddle'll do grand."

So thus on the next day, when the staghounds met at the "Black Bull," Tally Ho and Puddle—a gaunt brown, called that because of the hollow in his thin back—were both present. Their rider, W. Sorrel, Esq., turned out in a brown tweed outfit with an old worn hunting-cap on his head. As they waited around at the meet he spoke thus to a friend:

"Yes, I got a second horse out. These hirelings? Never. This here gee is aged four. T'other un five. Wot age did ye take 'em fur? Twelve, fourtin, fiftin, twenty? Heh! These here are thoroughbreds. Sire, n'arab, dam racehorse. Wot? Did I say they were thoro'breds. I did, an' so th'are. Heh!"

Thus he spoke in his ignorance, and when the carted stag was well away he started off at full gallop, down a ride heading him back again. Heedless of the master's "Hold hard!" he crammed at a great bank. The grey saw that he would land on a hound and swerved in the air. But if he did miss the hound he unseated his rider, who fell floundering into the muddy ditch on the far side.

"Horse has more sense than the rider," muttered a muddy

gentleman, tramping across a field. "Wish someone would catch my horse. Ah, here comes that grey again! Whoe there —who-e." The gentleman reached out and caught Tally Ho's reins, and suddenly acting on a wicked impulse, he vaulted on to the horse's back. As he galloped off he laughed at the funny sight of W. Sorrel, Esq., scrambling helplessly out of the ditch, for he was only a young fellow and the situation tickled him. "Anyhow, he is too much of a fool to ride the horse," remarked the sinner, "but hasn't he some bellows to mend, though! Why, both horse and rider need 'em patched up. . . ."

That stag was the spirit of speed in reality. Hounds ran him up hill and down dale at a pace which left few in the van. The grey horse was flagging now. He was blowing like a steam-engine and was bathed in a sweat of foam and lather. Luckily his rider was a good one, and after having nearly come to grief over a large bank he pulled up.

"Well, laddie, I think we have had enough now."

Tally Ho started at the words, and a hazy recollection flitted across his brain. He knew the voice well and yet he could not place it. As that voice spoke on softly that recollection came and went. And yet he could not lay a hold on it. Then it came in a flash, just as his rider yelled "Go on" to a friend in distress. There was no mistaking, that voice belonged to no other than Leslie Hamilton!

But Tally Ho's joy was short-lived, for the next instant an agony swept across his brain. An agony that only dumb animals know. "Oh, if only I could make him understand!" The grey did not fully realise this, but a vague idea lurked in his mind that if only Leslie knew the state of affairs— recognised him—he would not be returning to the cheerless comfort of the livery stables. He had a hasty vision of a cosy

75

stable, deep rustling straw, a warm gruel, soft bran-mash, and . . .

"Here is my car at last," exclaimed Leslie. "And, by Jove! here's your master, you horse." And sure enough there was W. Sorrel, Esq., on Puddle, limping along the moonlit road.

"Got mah horse, you there, ye . . ."

"Noodle!" suggested Leslie. "Yes, here he is, all neat and trim. By the way, where does he come from?"

"Dublin."

"When did they buy him?" Leslie paused on the step of his car, while his eyes wandered with a glance of interest, even with a slight gleam of recognition, to the old grey.

"Wot's that got t'do with you?"

"Oh, all right! Excuse me, won't you? Ta ta."

And a moment later a big car was speeding along the shiny glassy road and an old grey horse was trudging along on the weary ride home.

# CHAPTER XXIII: *CHANGES*

A friend in need
Is a friend indeed.
A PROVERB.

CHANGES they were and great changes. The sun shone as before over the busy humming city of Dublin; the old river "Liffy" glided along between her two thick walls just the same; the long line of carts pulled by heavy draught-horses or minute grey donkeys trundled along as they used to do, while the old tower of St. Mickan's still pealed forth its merry Christmas cheer, for that season had come round once more.

Where were the changes?

In an ancient wooden shack in an old cobbled street stood a grey horse. If Major Smithfield could have seen him now he would never have recognised his favourite, for his dapple coat, almost white now, was dull and staring; all his beautiful silky flowing mane that Atly used to take such a pride in was hogged away, while his long and swishing tail was docked. This, however, was not all. His eyes looked dull and listless, his legs were puffed and filled from overwork, and his ribs and hips stuck out from lack of condition. He was old, too, now . . . . fourteen summers had slipped behind him . . . for four years had passed since that last hunt. The proud, bold, grey hunter of yesterday, and the weary, old, white hireling of to-day.

Mr. Fink had retired from work leaving his son to go on

77

with the business. This son was a much worse man than his father, for besides possessing an awful temper, he also possessed a love for drink, and as Dapple heard his harsh voice giving orders in the yard, he shuddered, and remembered the advice that he had craved from the old dust-cart cob three and a half years ago. " 'Tis an evil day for you, Dapple," the old pony had said, "when that brute becomes your master, for the creature has no mercy. But don't rebel, it doesn't pay. I have tried it myself and I know. We animals must just hang on until the end." Tally Ho had often pondered on his words, for they all had their meaning. But he had not seen the pony about lately, for another pony had taken his place in the rubbish cart; and though Tally Ho was ignorant of the fact, the old cob had dropped down dead between his shafts and thus was put out of his misery.

But Tally Ho had his friends, human or otherwise, and good friends they were too. There was Freddie and Coral and Silvertail—those were his greatest companions—and Topsie and Hoolie and Skittles. Freddie was the son of the head boy and a kinder or merrier child there never was. This little chap of seven was the grey's favourite, " 'Coz he knowed me first," as Freddie put it. His family lived over the stables, and thus in his free time he always came down to "play wiv" Dapple. The grey always had loved children and Freddie always had loved horses and so they got on very well. Coral was an old, weedy-looking arab who was called "Bill" by human beings, but in respect for the poor old fellow's feelings Tally Ho called him Coral, for that was his real name in his old Egyptian home. Coral was an interesting animal, for he had travelled nearly all the way round the world—at different times—and knew a great many strange countries. Silvertail was a young grey horse who had also hunted a lot and thus

78

became fast friends with our grey. Topsie was a funny little black pony who Dapple sometimes met outside. Hoolie was a mongrel puppy and Skittles was the fluffiest of kittens.

But it was Christmas Day now and there could be no mistake about that. The shops were decked out in Father Christmases and gay Christmas hangings. The streets were crowded with carts and drays and people were rushing around in a great hurry over different things. And then at 11.30, a time when all good folk were in church, and all bad folk—like Mr. Fink—were in the public-house, Freddie entered the gloomy shed where Tally Ho was, carrying a branch of mistletoe in his hand and a great blanket over his head, followed by Skittles playfully fleeing from the rascal Hoolie in the rear. When everyone was inside Freddie shut the door and gravely climbed on the manger to tie the mistletoe to a beam, talking softly all the while.

"Faix, Dapple, d'ye not know that it be Christmas Day? Well, it is to be shure, d'ye see? Dapple, y'ain't attendin'! Listen now, it's Christ . . . Stop, Hoolie, ye! Yer after playin' wiv Dapple's feet! Well, it's Christmas. . . . Lookit, Skittles, yer will be kilt! Mind now!" as the adventurous kitten jumped on to the horse's back, "well, it's Chri . . . Oh, bad cess t'ye all, ye can't listen!"

With that Freddie jumped into the straw, and having lifted the kitten down he threw the blanket over Tally Ho's shivering body, and took the soft muzzle between his tiny hands and kissed it, there, under the mistletoe. By this time Coral's wise face appeared over the partition on one side, while Topsie's black muzzle appeared on the other. Freddie ran to kiss each and then said:

"Listen, all of ye. That blanket Dapple's got, *I* stole it. Sh! Don't tell! Ar stole this, too. Look now!" With that he

79

lifted up his jersey and out fell a cake, some sweets, a tin box containing some corn, and a box of fudge. All the horses liked the look of it and licked their chops. "And," cried Freddie, clapping his hands, "it's *all* for *us*. Every bit of it! Sh-h—listen!"

Steps were heard outside the door, it was flung back and there, confronting them, stood Mr. Fink. There was a silence, and then the man spoke. "So," he snarled, "is this where ma food and clothin' goes to? Git out ye." He aimed a savage kick at poor Hoolie, who, with the kitten, went flying into the yard. The man was very much the worse for drink and spoke in a thick voice.

"Git out ye," he cried, turning to Freddie, and as the poor little fellow lingered looking at the trampled fudge on the floor, the man struck him across the face with the heavy butt of his riding-whip. The little chap gave a low moan, and at this a madness shot through Tally Ho's whole frame; he bared his teeth, laid back his ears, and kicked out with all his might and main. His aim was true, for he hit the man hard in the ribs. With a cry the man staggered back into the arms of a stableman and Freddie rushed out of the stable. In aiming one last kick at the world in general Tally Ho encountered a stone wall, a great pain shot up his off hind leg and he stood still and listened.

Someone—a stranger—entered the yard, and having taken in the situation in a moment, he entered Tally Ho's box, walked fearlessly up to him and patted him on the neck. Then, to the amazement of all the spectators, the old horse cocked his ears and gave a feeble neigh.

## CHAPTER XXIV: *HOW IT ENDED*

Sweetest Earth, I love and love thee.
Seas about thee, skies above thee,
   Sun and storms,
   Hues and forms
Of the clouds with floating shadows
On thy mountains and thy meadows.
MARGARET L. WOODS.

TOM HOWARD laid down the ten shillings on the table. "D'ye think that's enough?" he asked.

"Why, begorrah! The master, if he recovers, will be only a wantin' th' price o' th' bhrute's skin," laughed the head boy. "For my part, ar have no wish for hisself to live afther the way he treated my Fred."

"'Twas a great shame," agreed the kindly stranger. "But I mus' go and look to my buy." So Tom went into the stable, and while he was harnessing the old grey—for the only bridle he had was one with blinkers on—he gave a start and stood quite still. All that he could say was "Faix now!" and "Glory be to God"—and he kept on repeating this. And then, "Well, if that don't beat all! Look now, who had this big lump on his throat but that hoss down in Mayo. Colour, grey, size, legs, all right. Why 'tis him then! Oh, d'ye not remember Tom, the stable-boy?" And indeed this tall, strong, kind-looking man was no other than Tom, not only that either, but Farmer O'Neil had retired and Tom was now "boss" of the whole farm.

On leading Tally Ho out of the yard Tom noticed that

the horse was no longer going sound, in fact he was dead lame. But "Mayo for you and I, lad," cried the young man, patting him joyfully. And Mayo it was.

\* \* \* \* \*

The long train journey came to an end at last, and the old long-forgotten farm was reached. It was springtime and so he was put out in the field for the night. The long field, with the river running through the corner and the trees surrounding it, the hay against the wooden fence and far beyond the great iron gate, the wild brown bog. It was the field where, as a youngster, he had first been caught in days gone by.

It was as the golden sun set that he raised his head and breathed in the pure air of heaven, and as he gazed over the great brown waste-land he faintly heard a pony neigh. That was the challenge of freedom—the call of the wild, and what animal can withstand that? The old grey backed away from the gate, gathered up his tired limbs, and cleared the four-foot-six iron in one great bound. Once safely over, Tally Ho, the great hunter, was thrown to the winds and the wild Mayo gelding of former days returned.

At last he found the herd, found them standing by an old wizened and gnarled bush sprouting on the side of a hill, and though he did not know it, it was there as a woolly black foal that he had first entered into the world.

\* \* \* \* \*

The next morning when Tom came down to fetch him and found the field empty he guessed what had happened.

"Let him bide there," he said, "for he has deserved it." And indeed he had.

\* \* \* \* \*

Now the grey is very happy, for he is the undisputed master of the herd and leads them at will.

But sometimes, when a far-off motor hoots or a distant curlew calls, he will raise his head from the grass and listen. For he still thinks and believes that one day the hounds and horses will come thundering down the slopes and that once again the horn will sound and the "Gone Away" and "Tally —ho" will re-echo through the silent woods at dawn.

The Westminster Press
411A Harrow Road
London W.9